THE RAINBOW CIRCUS

a truly brilliant show

BIG SHOW TONIGHT!

The Rainbow Circus Comes to Town

by JOANNE RYDER
Illustrated by BARBARA STEIDMAN

A GOLDEN BOOK • NEW YORK
Western Publishing Company, Inc., Racine, Wisconsin 53404

The circus is coming to town. The big parade is about to begin!

Two boys ride blue unicycles up the street. They are carrying the big circus sign. As they wheel slowly by, the blue feathers in their blue caps wave in the wind.

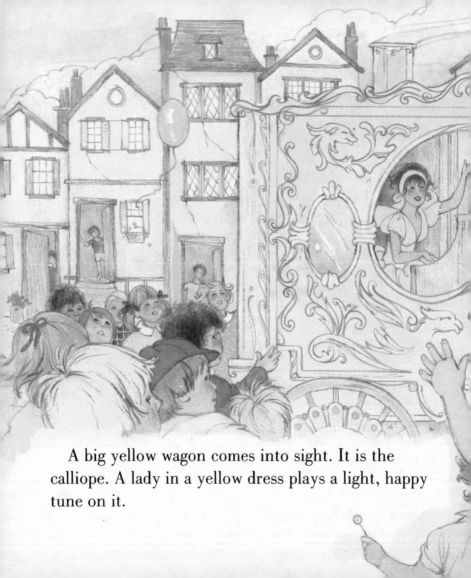

A big yellow wagon comes into sight. It is the calliope. A lady in a yellow dress plays a light, happy tune on it.

A family of tumblers somersault down the street next. They are all dressed in red. A young girl with bright red hair does a handstand.

Then a clown in a green suit chases a clown in an orange dress down the street.

The clown in the green suit stops and reaches inside his big green coat pocket. He pulls out a green balloon and hands it to a little boy.

Then the clown in the orange dress stops and reaches inside a big orange purse. He pulls out a bunch of orange flowers and throws them into the crowd.

The animal acts come next.

Three huge gray elephants walk slowly by, waving their long trunks.

Six small white dogs leap down the street. A girl in a white dress holds up a white hoop. The dogs jump through the hoop again and again.

A young girl dressed in a black suit balances on
the back of a beautiful black horse.

The parade is almost over. Only the jugglers are left. They are dressed in purple and are juggling purple balls.

A carriage comes by carrying a tall lady in a
rainbow-colored dress. She is the ringmaster of the
Rainbow Circus.

"I hope you enjoyed our parade," she calls.
"Come tonight and see the Truly Brilliant Show."

That night the circus performs in the big rainbow-colored tent. The lady in the rainbow-colored dress introduces all the acts.

The two boys ride their blue unicycles around the ring.

The white dogs jump through hoops, and the gray elephants balance balls.

Everyone laughs when the clown in the orange dress pours water on the clown in the green suit.

The red-haired girl tumbles on a trampoline with her family.

The lady in the black suit rides around the ring on her beautiful black horse.

The jugglers toss purple balls high in the air, and the lady in the yellow dress plays the calliope.

What a Truly Brilliant Show the Rainbow Circus is!